Aviva's Piano

BY MIRIAM CHAIKIN
PICTURES BY YOSSI ABOLAFIA

CLARION BOOKS

TICKNOR & FIELDS: A HOUGHTON MIFFLIN COMPANY

NEW YORK

*To Noga Gibbs, Ella Gaffen,
and the children at Kfar Giladi.*

Clarion Books
Ticknor & Fields, a Houghton Mifflin Company
Text copyright © 1986 by Miriam Chaikin
Illustrations copyright © 1986 by Yossi Abolafia

Library of Congress Cataloging-in-Publication Data
Chaikin, Miriam.
Aviva's piano.
Summary: Aviva's piano is too large to fit
through the door of her home on the kibbutz, until a
terrorist's bomb provides an unexpected solution.
[1. Collective settlements—Israel—Fiction.
2. Israel—Fiction.   3. Piano—Fiction]
I. Abolafia, Yossi, ill.   II. Title.
PZ7.C3487Av   1986   [E]   85-13325
ISBN 0-89919-367-6

Y   10   9   8   7   6   5   4   3   2   1

Contents

About the Story   1

1. The Piano Comes   3

2. Late for Class   12

3. Down to the Shelter   19

4. All-Clear!   28

5. A Hole in the Wall   33

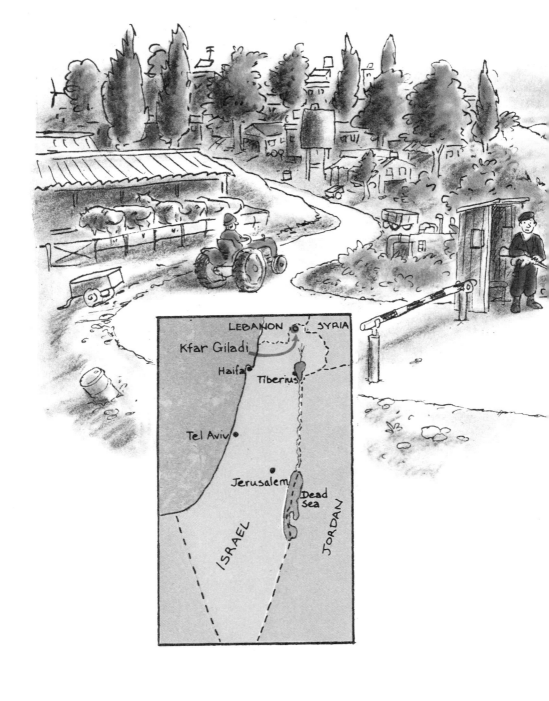

LEBANON SYRIA

Kfar Giladi

Haifa

Tiberius

Tel Aviv

Jerusalem

Dead
Sea

ISRAEL

JORDAN

About the Story

Aviva lives on Kfar Giladi in Israel. Kfar Giladi is a kibbutz in the north of the country, near the border of Lebanon.

Kfar means ''village'' in Hebrew, and this kibbutz is much like any village. The children go to school on the kibbutz. Their parents work there. They raise cotton, grow apples or avocados, breed fish, work at the dairy, or do other things. Everyone knows everyone else.

But a kibbutz is also very different from a village. For example, Aviva's mother works at the kibbutz hotel. Her father works at the stone quarry. Yet they earn no money. Instead, they receive whatever they need to live—an apartment, food, furniture and clothing for the family.

Like most people who live on the kibbutz, Aviva and her parents are Jews. They used to live in Argentina until they began to feel unwelcome there. So they moved to Israel, which is a Jewish country. Now they feel more at home.

Aviva and the other children spend the whole day at a children's house. There is one for each age group. Aviva is in the third grade. In Children's House 3, she goes to school, has her meals, rests and plays. At the end of the day, when her parents are finished working, she heads for home.

Each children's house has a schoolroom, rooms with beds and shelves for each child, a bathroom with showers, a large kitchen, and a bomb shelter.

1

The Piano Comes

The weekend was over. It was Sunday morning and the start of a new week. Aviva got ready for school. She put her sweater and book in her *tiq*, her tote bag. There was a rumbling noise outside, and she stopped to listen. It was a truck, but not a kibbutz truck. She knew the sound the kibbutz trucks made. She heard the truck come to a halt in front of her house.

"Aviva! Come quick!" her mother said, looking out the window.

Aviva ran to the window. So did her father. They looked down.

Aviva clapped her hands together. "My piano!" she cried.

"So it is," her father said.

Aviva, her mother, and father watched as the driver and his helper jumped up into the back of the truck, where the piano was.

Aviva hugged herself. "*Oi*—I can't believe

it," she said. "I thought it would never come."

"You see," her mother said. "You worried for nothing. We told you it was coming."

Aviva turned to her mother. "You told me when we left Buenos Aires it was on a boat to Israel," she said.

"It was," said her mother.

"When we lived with Aunt Esther in Tel Aviv, you told me it would be here any day," Aviva said.

"That's what the moving company told us," Aviva's father said.

Aviva turned to her father. "When we moved here, you still said it would be here any day," she said.

"Well—that's what they told us," her father said.

"We moved here in the winter. Now it's spring," Aviva said.

"Don't blame us," her father said with a shrug.

"Why are we standing up here?" Aviva's mother said. "Let's go down and see the piano."

Aviva, her mother, and her father ran down the stairs.

The driver and his helper had removed the

piano from the truck.

"What took you so long to get here?" Aviva asked.

"There was a lot of traffic on the road," the driver said.

Aviva went up to the piano. She touched it. She struck a note. She put her arms around the piano, as far as they would go. "I can't believe it," she said.

The driver stood looking up at Aviva's window. He shifted his gaze to the door. He took a folding yardstick from his pocket.

Aviva's parents beamed as she walked around the piano one way, touching it, while the driver walked around the piano the other way, measuring it. Aviva and her parents watched as the driver then went to measure the door.

"I need to measure the window," he said.

"Come, I'll take you upstairs," Aviva's father said.

Aviva, her mother, and the helper stood looking up, watching the man measure the window. Behind them, the lanes began to fill with people. Children were carrying their *tiqs*,

heading for school. Grown-ups were going to work. Everyone called ''Hello'' or ''Good Morning'' to Aviva and her mother. A neighbor called, ''Welcome, Mr. Piano!''

The driver and Aviva's father came down. The driver scratched his head and measured the piano again.

"So?" his helper said.

The driver growled and made a face. "I hate to tell you," he said to Aviva and her parents. "But the piano will not go in."

Aviva thought the ground under her would open up. "Not go in?" she repeated.

"The door is too small," the driver said. "The window also. The piano will not go in." He shook his head.

Aviva's eyes filled with tears as she turned to look first at her mother then at her father.

"Aviva!" a voice called from the lane.

Aviva knew it was Rakeli. Rakeli was her best friend. They were in Children's House 3 together. Aviva blinked the tears from her eyes and faced the lane.

"So it finally arrived," Rakeli said.

Aviva sniffled.

"Are you coming to school or not?" Rakeli asked.

Aviva glanced at the piano then turned back to Rakeli. "No!" she said.

"The teacher hates lateness," Rakeli said.

"I don't care," Aviva said.

"Well, I don't want to be late," Rakeli said, hurrying up the lane.

2

Late for Class

Rakeli was glad she had seen Aviva's piano. The first class on Sunday was "talk lesson." Children who had something to tell about the weekend told it. Nothing special had happened to Rakeli over the weekend. When she left home, she was sorry she had nothing to tell. Now she could tell about Aviva's piano.

At Children's House 3, Rakeli hung up her *tiq* on the hook marked with her name. Before going into the schoolroom, she stuck her head into the kitchen-dining room. She was hungry and was glad to see that Varda, the *metapelet* who made the meals, was preparing breakfast.

"*Boker tov*, good morning," Rakeli called inside.

"*Boker tov*," Varda answered.

Rakeli hurried on into the classroom and took her seat.

Irit, the teacher, stood in front of the room.

"I see that Rami and Aviva are not here," she said, glancing about. "*Tov*, all right, we'll begin without them. Who has something to tell?"

Rakeli and Joshua waved their hands in the air.

"Joshua," Irit said.

"Yesterday," Joshua began, "a boy was here from a kibbutz near Tiberias." He slapped his head. "I couldn't believe it," he said. "They don't have a bomb shelter on his kibbutz!"

"It's not surprising," Irit said. "Who knows why?" she asked, glancing about at the raised hands.

Rakeli wasn't sure of the answer so she raised her hand but kept it close to the desk.

"Nofar!" Irit said.

"We are on the Lebanon border," Nofar said. "The *katyusha* rockets that the terrorists fire from Lebanon can reach us. But the rockets can't reach Tiberias. It's too far away. That's why they don't need shelters there."

"*Tov*," Irit said. She glanced about. "Who else has something to tell?"

Rakeli waved and waved her hand. "Irit, call

on me, please!'' she said.

"Rakeli," Irit said.

"Aviva's piano came," Rakeli said. "I just saw it. It's standing in front of her house," she added, to make the report longer.

Just then Rami came rushing in.

"Why are you late?" Irit asked.

"Aviva's crying," Rami said as he took his seat.

"Why should that make *you* late?" Irit asked.

"I had to find out why she was crying, didn't I?" Rami said. "In case she needed help," he added.

"*Tov*, in that case, suppose you share the information with us. Why *was* Aviva crying?"

"Her piano came, but it won't go in the house," Rami said.

In the next moment, Aviva herself came shuffling in. Her eyes were red from crying. Aviva's seat was next to Rakeli. She walked over to the empty seat and sat down.

"*Boker tov*, good morning, Aviva," Irit said. "It's 'talk lesson' time. We heard about your piano from Rakeli and Rami. Would you like to tell us about it too?"

Aviva was annoyed to hear that others had talked about *her* piano during "talk lesson."

She wiped her eyes. "After all the waiting for it to come, it won't go in," she said, sniffling. "The door is too small. The window, too."

Suddenly the loudspeaker began to crackle. Aviva blinked her eyes dry and sat up to listen.

The crackling meant an announcement was coming. It could just be someone in the office looking for someone in the dairy, or in the rock quarry. Or it could be something more important. It could be an alert.

''ATTENTION! ATTENTION! EVERYONE TO THE SHELTER!'' the voice on the loudspeaker said.

It *was* an alert. The Israeli soldiers stationed on the border must have seen terrorists in Lebanon preparing to fire *katyusha* rockets. So they had notified the kibbutz scout by walkie-talkie.

Aviva and the children stood up. They had been through other alerts.

''*Tov*,'' Irit said. ''No running. No pushing. No noise. Line up two-by-two, hold hands, and follow me.''

3

Down to the Shelter

Aviva and Rakeli were first in line, behind Irit. Was it a real alert? Aviva wondered. Sometimes it was a false alarm. Aviva hoped it was a false alarm.

Irit glanced over her shoulder, to the back of the line. "Varda, are you with us?" she said.

"I'm here," Varda answered from the back.

Irit opened the door of the children's house and went outside. The door of the shelter was just a few steps away. Aviva and Rakeli and the other children followed Irit down the stairs to the shelter. It was underground.

The shelter was exactly like the children's house, except that it had no windows. The shelter, too, had a schoolroom, rooms with beds for children, and a kitchen-dining room.

Aviva took her same seat as upstairs, beside Rakeli. The other children did the same. Irit sat at a desk in front. Varda sat near her, on a bench.

Now that she was seated in the shelter, along with the other children, Aviva thought more about the alert. She knew she was safe underground and that no harm could come to her in the shelter. Even so, she did not like the idea of falling rockets. And she hated the howling sound they made—*whu! whu! whu!*—as they sped through the air.

"*Tov*, does anyone have anything else to tell?" Irit asked.

Joshua raised his hand.

"You already told something," Irit said.

"I know," he said. "But that boy in Tiberias—what if the rocket *could* reach his kibbutz? They have no shelter!"

"But it can't. Tiberias is too far," Irit said. "Now who else?"

Aviva knew her parents were safe. There were shelters all over the kibbutz. As soon as an alert was sounded, everyone ran into the nearest shelter. Even so, she wanted to hear Irit say so. She raised her hand.

"Aviva?"

"It's not about the 'talk lesson,' " Aviva said.

"*Tov*, tell it anyway," Irit said.

"It's a question," Aviva said.

"Very well, ask it."

"Are the mothers and fathers in the shelters?" Aviva asked.

"Of course," Irit said. "All parents are in one of the shelters. Everyone is underground—and safe."

Aviva thought about her piano. It was standing in front of the house. If the alert was real, the piano would not be safe. A piano cannot run into a shelter.

She winced and stuck her fingers in her ears.

The alert was real. Even with her fingers in her ears she could hear the awful howling—*whu! whu! whu!*—as the rockets flew by. BANG! She heard an explosion. That meant one of the rockets had landed someplace on the kibbutz. She hoped it wasn't anywhere near the piano.

Soon the rockets stopped and the howling ended. Aviva removed her fingers from her ears. The silence was nice. It did not mean the danger was over, though. There would be an all-clear signal on the loudspeaker when it was.

Rami raised his hand. "I'm hungry," he said. "We're supposed to have breakfast now."

"I'm hungry, too," Rakeli said.

Joshua, Nofar, and all the children began calling out that they were hungry. All except Aviva. She sat thinking about her piano.

Varda stood up. "No problem," she said. "Let's see what we have to eat in the kitchen. I'll just go get it." She looked around the room.

"Come help me, Joshua," she said.

Varda and Joshua disappeared into the kitchen. A few minutes later they came back carrying two trays. Varda and all the children followed them into the dining room. Irit too.

On the trays were orange slices and bread smeared with honey, enough for everyone.

"How many orange slices should we take?" Nofar asked.

"Two, three," Varda said. "If there are any left over, you can have more."

Each child took some orange slices and a slice of bread and sat down at a table to eat. Aviva also sat, but she ate nothing.

"You're not hungry?" Irit asked.

Aviva shook her head.

"Can I have your bread then?" Rakeli asked.

Aviva nodded.

Rakeli took Aviva's slice of bread from the tray.

The children sat talking and eating. Aviva sat in silence, wondering about her piano. When breakfast was over, everyone went back to the schoolroom.

4

All-Clear!

Irit opened a book on her desk.

"Children," she said, "we will have a read-aloud lesson. As I call your name, come to the front to read."

Aviva looked away. She did not want the teacher to call on her. She wanted to worry about her piano. A rocket had exploded. But where?

"What about our play, *Bible Days*," Nofar said. "We were supposed to have a rehearsal after breakfast. Sarah said so on Friday, before school ended."

"Yes, but as you see, things got changed around," Irit said. "Sarah is not here. She is in some other shelter. And she has the book. We can't have a rehearsal without Sarah—or the book.''

''Why not?'' Rami said. ''I know my part without the book. I'm supposed to be a sheep. When the shepherd stands near the well, I say *meeehh, meeehhh.*''

''I know my part, too,'' Joshua said. ''I'm a goat. I say *behhh, behhhh.*''

"I need the book. I'm a maiden at the well," Rakeli called. "I don't remember what I'm supposed to say to the shepherd."

"*Tov*," Irit said. "We need the book for other children as well."

Aviva needed the book, too. She played the mother of the maiden at the well. But she said nothing. She was still thinking about her piano.

Just then there was a crackling on the loudspeaker. It was the sound Aviva had been waiting for. She held her breath to listen.

"ATTENTION! ATTENTION! YOU MAY LEAVE THE SHELTERS!" the voice on the loudspeaker said.

The alert was over! There were rules to be followed. Aviva knew the rules. Children were supposed to remain seated until the teacher spoke. They were supposed to follow the teacher up the stairs. And they were supposed to remain in the children's house until their parents came to see them.

Aviva didn't care about the rules. She hurried from her seat and ran to the stairs.

"Aviva!" Irit called.

"I have to see if my piano is all right," Aviva said.

"The only thing you have to do is wait for your parents," Irit said. "They'll come here looking for you."

Aviva didn't like the sound of Irit's voice. She waited near the stairs.

Irit walked to the stairs. "*Tov*, take hands," she said to the children. "No running. No pushing. No noise. Understood?"

"Understood," Aviva answered with the other children.

5

A Hole in the Wall

Aviva and Rakeli, holding hands, stood behind Irit. The other children lined up behind them. All followed Irit up the stairs.

Everyone wanted to go outside and see where the rocket had fallen. Even though Irit had said, "no pushing," the children began to push while they were on the stairs. Aviva had to push back. It was the only way she could keep her place next to Irit and remain first in line.

Upstairs, Irit opened the door. Aviva blinked against the daylight. Irit made a gate with her arms, to hold the children back and keep them from running out. Aviva got under Irit's arm

and looked outside. She saw smoke where the
rocket had fallen. To her relief, her house was
in the opposite direction.

All the lanes were full of parents running to see their children in the different children's houses. Aviva did not see her parents among them.

Hemmy, the kibbutz driver, drove up in his car. He was Irit's boyfriend.

"What got hit?" Irit asked, nodding toward the smoke.

"It exploded in the field, near the dairy," Hemmy said.

"Any damage?" Irit asked.

"A cow got killed," Hemmy said.

Aviva was sorry for the cow but glad her piano was safe.

"Any other damage?" Irit asked.

"Nothing serious," Hemmy said. He glanced up the lane. "One of the rockets grazed a house and knocked a hole in the wall."

Aviva winced. She lived up that way. Which house? What wall? Rule or no rule, she was not going to wait for her parents to arrive. She dashed out from under Irit's arm and ran up the lane. She heard Irit call after her, but she kept on running.

It *was* her house that the rocket had grazed. The downstairs was fine. But upstairs, where she lived, part of the wall had been knocked out. Pieces of wall lay on the ground. The window frame lay at her feet. But the piano was safe! A little dusty, but safe. Aviva blew dust from the piano, lifted the cover, and hit a few keys.

Her mother and father came running.

"Oh!" her mother said, seeing the wall.

"Ugh!" her father said.

They turned to Aviva. "Aviva! We went to the children's house looking for you," her mother said, taking Aviva in her arms.

"I had to see if the piano was all right," Aviva said.

Aviva's father lifted her up for a squeeze and put her back down again.

"Did you see the wall?" Aviva asked.

"We saw it..." Aviva's mother and father said, looking first at the hole then at the pieces of wall on the ground.

People on the lanes called out to them.

''So—it was your house that was grazed!'' someone said.

''Too bad!'' another said.

''It could have been worse,'' Aviva's mother

answered over her shoulder.

"I'll get some men to come and help me clear up the mess," Aviva's father said.

"Better go to the office first," Aviva's mother said. "We need a new wall. They'll have to send carpenters and plasterers."

Aviva's father nodded.

Aviva's face broke into a smile as she gazed down at the window at her feet. "Mother! Father!" she said.

Her parents looked at her.

"The window was too small. But there is no window now," Aviva said. She pointed at the hole in the wall. "Now the piano will go in!"

"You're right," her mother said.

"So it will," her father said. "I'll get the truck with the pulleys, too," he said, heading for the office.

"Oooo!" Aviva said, hugging herself with joy. Something good had come from something bad.

Aviva's father and his friends removed the
pieces of wall that had fallen inside and outside
the house. Aviva helped her mother sweep up
inside.

The truck with pulleys came and lifted the piano up and into the house through the missing wall. The plasterers and carpenters worked on the wall until it got dark. Part of the wall was still missing, though.

It was too cold to sleep in the house, so that night, Aviva, her mother, and father slept in Children's House 3. Aviva had a happy dream about her piano, safe now in the living room.